A Pony in Trouble

Do you love ponies? Be a Pony Pal!

Look for these Pony Pal books:

Pony Pal #1 I Want a Pony

Pony Pal #2 A Pony for Keeps

coming soon

Pony Pal #4 Give Me Back My Pony

Pony Pals

A Pony in Trouble

Jeanne Betancourt

illustrated by Paul Bachem

A
LITTLE APPLE
PAPERBACK

SCHOLASTIC INC.
New York Toronto London Auckland Sydney

ISBN 0-590-48585-7

Text copyright © 1995 by Jeanne Betancourt.
Illustrations copyright © 1995 by Scholastic Inc.
All rights reserved. Published by Scholastic Inc.
APPLE PAPERBACKS ® is a registered trademark of Scholastic Inc.

24 23 22 21 20 19 18 17   9/9 0/0

Printed in the U.S.A.   40

First Scholastic printing, March 1995

For Ryan

The author thanks Dr. Kent Kay for medical consultation on this story.

Thanks also to Elvia Gignoux and Helen Perelman for their editorial assistance.

Contents

1. A Beautiful Morning — 1
2. The Mystery Illness — 8
3. Choosing a Color — 17
4. Not Again! — 26
5. Pony Watch — 34
6. The Racing Bike — 42
7. Stop! — 51
8. The Gift — 61
9. The Chicken-Pox Horse Show — 71
10. Don't Stop! — 80
11. The Parade — 87

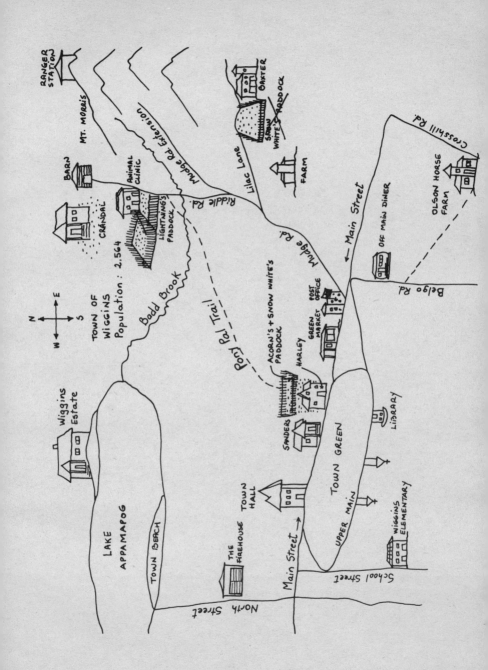

A Pony in Trouble

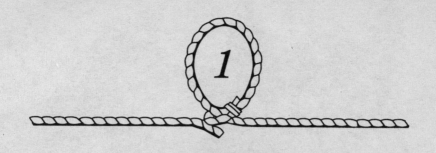

A Beautiful Morning

Pam Crandal woke up to her dog's loud bark. The family dog, Woolie, slept in the kitchen. Early in the morning when he was let out into the yard, his bark was Pam's wake-up call.

Pam got out of bed and looked out the window to the paddock below. Her chestnut-colored pony, Lightning, was standing under the big sugar maple tree. That's where the pony spent the night. Lightning was watching the dog dashing around the paddock. She neighed at Woolie as if to

say, "Good Morning. What's all the fuss about?"

Pam dressed and had a bowl of cereal before she went out to feed Lightning. When the pony saw Pam, she galloped toward her. By the time Pam opened the paddock gate, Lightning was there to greet her with a gentle nudge on the shoulder. Pam returned the greeting with a good-morning hug around the pony's neck.

"It's spring vacation," she told Lightning. "That means we'll be together all day long."

Pam gave Lightning fresh water to drink and some oats and hay. "Eat up," she told her pony. "We're going on a big trail ride today."

Pam left Lightning and went to the barn to do all her morning chores. Winter was finally over and a whole week of spring vacation lay ahead. She knew that her best friends, Anna Harley and Lulu Sanders, were doing their barn chores, too. When they were finished, Anna and Lulu would ride over to Pam's on their ponies, Acorn and Snow White. They'd take the mile-and-a-half path through the woods connecting Pam's house and Anna's house. The three friends called it Pony Pal Trail.

Pam was on her way out of the barn when she noticed a poster on her mother's barn-office door. She went up to the door to get a better look. WIGGINS HORSE SHOW, the poster announced.

Pam was reading the poster when she felt a hand on her shoulder. Pam jumped. She looked up to see her mother standing beside her.

"Sorry I scared you, honey," Mrs. Crandal said. "I thought you heard me come in." She pointed to the poster. "Didn't the poster for the horse show come out nice?"

"It looks great," Pam said.

"It's really a shame that you don't enter Lightning in horse shows," Mrs. Crandal said. "I picked her out especially because I knew she'd be a great show pony for you."

Pam remembered the day two years ago when her parents drove her to Echo Farm to pick out a Connemara pony. She'd tried two other ponies before Mr. Echo brought over Lightning. In a few turns around the ring, Pam knew that Lightning was perfectly trained.

After that first ride, Pam studied Lightning's face. That's when she noticed that the white marking on the pony's forehead was shaped like an upside-down heart. She also noticed the alert, friendly look in Lightning's dark eyes.

To Pam, Lightning seemed to be saying, "Come on. Take me home. You know we belong together." That's when Pam knew that she and this pony were meant for each other.

Pam turned to her mother, "You didn't pick out Lightning, Mom. I did."

"That's true," her mother said. "But I made sure we only looked at ponies that had good potential for showing. I wish you'd let Lightning show off what she can do."

Competing in horse shows was something that Pam and her mother disagreed about a lot. Mrs. Crandal thought that being in a horse show was a big deal. As a riding teacher she worked hard preparing kids to be in horse shows. Pam felt that her mother was disappointed in her for not being in them. But she couldn't help it. She hated horse shows.

"I didn't pick out Lightning because she could win a bunch of ribbons," Pam said.

"Being in horse shows is more than winning ribbons," her mother said.

"Well, I just don't like them," Pam said.

"I'll bet your friends will want to be in the show," Mrs. Crandal said. "Snow White is such a good jumper. And I figured that Anna would be excited that the show is at Reggie Olson's farm where she bought Acorn."

Pam didn't tell her mother that she hadn't told her friends about the horse show. Instead she said, "None of us like horse shows. We're going trail riding all week."

Just then Pam heard the sound of horses'

6

hooves. Through the open barn door she could see Anna and Lulu galloping toward her on their ponies.

"Come quickly!" Anna shouted. "Something's wrong with Lightning."

Pam ran ahead of her mother and past her friends into the paddock. In a far corner she saw Lightning pawing the ground and kicking. Pam raced across the paddock toward her pony.

She knew something was terribly wrong.

The Mystery Illness

"What's wrong, Lightning?" Pam asked.

For a split second Lightning raised her head and looked at Pam. Pam saw pain and fear in her pony's eyes. It was a look that shouted "Help me." The moment passed and Lightning lowered her head again and tried to kick her own stomach.

Pam's father was a veterinarian who ran a clinic for large animals. So Pam had been around sick horses all her life. Now, for the first time, her *own* pony was the one in trouble.

Lulu and Anna rode up beside Pam.

"What's wrong with her?" Lulu asked.

"I think it's her stomach," Pam answered.

"Your mother's gone to get your father," Anna said.

Pam told Lightning, "Dad'll be here in a minute. He'll know what to do to help you."

Pam thought of what else had to be done. She told Lulu, "We'll need a halter and a lead rope."

"Okay," Lulu said. She turned Snow White around and cantered back toward the barn to get one.

Pam turned to Anna, "For now you'd better put Acorn in the other paddock. And Snow White, too, when Lulu comes back." Pam was relieved to see her father and mother rushing across the paddock.

A few minutes later, Pam's father told the Pony Pals what Pam had already guessed. "Lightning has colic," he said. Pam knew that colic was an upset stomach and problems in the intestines. She also knew that horses could die from colic.

"Ponies hardly ever throw up because of the way their stomachs are built," Pam said to Lulu.

"I know," Lulu said sadly.

Pam remembered the time she'd got food poisoning from spoiled mayonnaise at a picnic. It was the worst upset stomach she'd ever had. For a whole day she had terrible cramps. She threw up over and over again. What would have happened if she hadn't been able to get rid of what was making her sick?

"We worm her regularly," Dr. Crandal said, "so I don't think it's a parasite." He gave Lightning two shots. One was a pain-killer. The other was to help her digestion.

"What has she been eating?" Mrs. Crandal asked.

"Oats and hay," Pam told her mother.

"How much?" Dr. Crandal asked.

Pam cupped her hand and put it out. "A handful of oats. And two flakes of hay. Like always," she said.

"That shouldn't cause this trouble. Better check that hay to be sure it isn't moldy," he said.

Pam felt awful. Had she made her own pony sick?

"Let's get her to walk around a little," Dr. Crandal said.

While her father held Lightning's head, Pam quickly slipped on the halter. "We're going to help you," she told Lightning. Then, more to herself than the pony, she added, "Be brave."

"Now walk her," Dr. Crandal directed.

Pam attached the lead rope to the halter. Lulu and Anna stood on either side of Pam. Now Lightning could see all three Pony Pals.

"Come on Lightning," Anna cooed. "Come with us."

"You can do it," urged Lulu. "We're all here to help you get better."

"Trust me," Pam told her pony. "I wouldn't ask you to do anything that wasn't good for you."

She pulled on the rope. Lightning moved a few steps forward. Pam and Lulu walked backward as they continued their encouraging words. And the pony continued to walk.

Dr. Crandal watched Lightning a while longer. "You girls are doing fine here with her," he said. "Keep her walking. Then we'll see how she's doing when the painkiller wears off."

Dr. Crandal went back to the animal clinic. Mrs. Crandal and Anna went into the barn to check if the hay was moldy. That left Pam and Lulu to walk Lightning.

"Thanks for helping, Lulu," Pam said as they led Lightning in a slow circle around the paddock.

As they walked her pony, Pam thought about how lucky she was to have two great best friends — Anna and Lulu.

Of the three Pony Pals, Anna was the most artistic. She loved to draw and to paint, especially pictures of horses. Anna was dyslexic, so reading and writing were hard for her. But that didn't mean she wasn't smart. Pam and Anna had been best friends since the day they met in kindergarten. Anna's mother owned the only diner in Wiggins — Off-Main Diner — and her father was a carpenter. He'd built the Crandals' barn.

Lulu's dad used to spend summers in Wiggins when he was a kid. Now his mother — Lulu's grandmother — lived in Wiggins all the time. And while Lulu's father was working in the Amazon jungle, Lulu was living with her grandmother in the house right next door to Anna. Best of all, Acorn and Snow White shared a paddock behind Anna's house.

It made Pam sad to remember that Lulu's mother had died when Lulu was little. But Pam knew that Lulu was very close to her father. They both loved the outdoors and adventure. Lulu's father was a naturalist who wrote about animals. He traveled for his work and usually took Lulu with him.

For two years, Lulu and her dad lived in England. Their cottage was right near a horse farm. That's where Lulu had taken riding lessons. Lulu knew almost as much about horses as Pam did.

"Pam," Lulu said, "look what Snow White and Acorn are doing."

Pam looked up to see the two ponies walking along the fence that separated them from Lightning. They were staying as close as possible to their friend.

"They're worried about her and want to keep her company," Lulu said.

Anna ran across the paddock toward Pam and Lulu. "The hay's not moldy," she told them. "So that's not what made Lightning sick."

"I wish I knew what did it," Pam said. "Then maybe I could keep it from happening again."

"Your dad said sometimes horses get sick and you never know why," Lulu said. Lulu patted Lightning on the neck. "I think she's going to be all right."

Anna gave Lightning a kiss on the cheek. "I think so, too."

But Pam couldn't help thinking, What if Lightning doesn't get better?

Choosing a Color

An hour later, Pam's father came out to check on Lightning. "She'll be okay," he told the girls.

The Pony Pals exchanged smiles of relief.

"Just let her rest today. And give her warm mash for supper," he said.

When Dr. Crandal left, Pam told her friends, "You guys go ahead and do the trail ride without Lightning and me." She looked up at the bright blue sky. "It's a great day for a ride."

"No, we'll hang out here today," Anna said.

"And have our picnic with you," Lulu added.

"I've got brownies from Mom's diner," Anna told them, "for all of us."

Pam's mouth watered as she remembered the delicious taste of Off-Main Diner's famous brownies. She was feeling more like herself now that she knew her pony was going to be okay. And she was glad her friends were going to stay with her.

"Let's brush Lightning," Anna suggested. "It'll help her relax."

Lulu and Anna led Lightning close to the barn while Pam ran ahead to get a grooming box. A few minutes later, the pony was sighing contentedly as the three girls petted and brushed her.

"I didn't know there was going to be a horse show at Olson's," Lulu said.

"A show?" Anna asked excitedly.

"I saw a poster for it on Mrs. Crandal's door," Lulu said. "When I got the harness."

Anna put down the currycomb. "Show me, Lulu," she said.

Pam was surprised that Anna was so interested. As her friends headed into the barn, Lulu turned and asked, "You coming, Pam?"

"I saw it already," Pam answered.

Through the open barn door Pam listened to Anna and Lulu reading the poster and talking about the show. "There's a Short Stirrup Division," Anna said. "That's perfect for me and Acorn."

"And a Pony Hunter Division that'll have a lot of jumping over fences," Lulu said. "That's just what Rema wants me to compete in with Snow White."

Pam, running her fingers through Lightning's mane, remembered that Snow White wasn't really Lulu's pony. Lulu was only taking care of the pretty white pony until her real owner, Rema Baxter, got home from boarding school in June. Lulu had to write reports to Rema telling her everything about Snow White.

When Anna and Lulu came back outside, Pam said, "Aren't horse shows dumb? Who would want to be showing off in front of a lot of people when you could be trail riding?"

"The neat thing about this show is that it's at Olson's farm," Anna said. "We can ride there. We don't have to borrow a horse trailer or anything."

"Snow White's a good jumper, so maybe we'll win some ribbons," Lulu put in. "Rema would like that."

"Rema's the sort of person who counts every ribbon she's won," Anna said.

Pam put her arms around Lightning's neck and gave the pony a hug. "I wouldn't ask Lightning to be in a show just so I could have a prize."

"I've only been in horse shows in England," Lulu said. "They were lots of fun whether I won ribbons or not. Aren't they fun in America, too?"

"I think so," Anna told Lulu. "I was in shows when I took lessons from Pam's mom. But I've never been in a show with Acorn." Anna turned to Pam. "Don't you think Acorn would have fun being in a horse show?"

"Acorn thinks trail riding is fun. Like us," Pam answered.

"But if we were all in the show," said Anna, "we would make it fun. We could all use the same color to decorate our ponies."

"It'd be our Pony Pal color," Lulu said.

Anna put her arm around Pam's shoulder. "Please, say you'll do it."

"*You* be in the horse show with Lulu," Pam told Anna. "But count me out."

"Pam, the show won't be the same if we don't all do it," Lulu said.

"Maybe you'll change your mind," Anna said.

"I won't," Pam insisted.

They were all quiet for a minute. This was the first time they were planning to do something that split them up. Pam knew it was her fault. But she couldn't help it.

"Let's have lunch," Lulu said, breaking the silence.

They put out an old horse blanket near the paddock. While they ate their sandwiches, they talked about how scary it was to have a sick pony. Then they talked about how much fun it was to trail ride. No one mentioned the horse show until they were eating the brownies.

"I think it'll be neat to have a Pony Pal color for the horse show," Anna said. "We can even decorate our riding sticks with the color we pick."

"And get yarn to braid in our ponies' manes," Lulu added. She looked from Anna to Pam. "So what should our color be?"

Anna pointed to the sky. "How about that shade of blue?" she asked. Lulu and Pam looked up. "It's called periwinkle blue," Anna explained.

"Perfect," Lulu said. "What do you think, Pam?"

"It's a pretty color," Pam said.

"Do you think it should be the Pony Pal color?" Anna asked.

"Sure. Why not?" Pam said. "But I'm still not going to be in the horse show. So don't ask me again, okay?"

"I wasn't asking you to be in the show," Anna pointed out. "Just if you voted yes for the color."

"Yes, I vote yes for the color," Pam said. She hated that her friends were trying to get her to be in a horse show. They're acting just like my mother, she thought.

"Come on, Lulu, let's go get the program and prize list from Mrs. Crandal," Anna said.

After they left, Pam decided that Lightning was ready to go in the big paddock with the other ponies. Lightning whinnied happily when she saw she was going to be let out with Acorn and Snow White.

"You didn't like being separated from your friends, did you?" she said to her pony. She leaned her head against Lightning's neck and sighed. "I'm beginning to know how that feels."

Not Again!

Early the next morning, Pam woke up to her bark-alarm. She smiled when she heard Lightning's cheerful neigh.

When Pam went out to the paddock, Lightning ran over to her and nudged her shoulder like always. That was a good sign, too. And after a drink of water, Lightning ate every last bite of her breakfast. Another good sign.

Before eating her own breakfast, Pam telephoned Lulu to tell her the good news. "Lightning's all better," she said. "Dad said I can take her out on a trail ride to-day."

"Great," Lulu said. "Anna and I are practicing with your mother for the horse show this morning. But after we finish, we'll go trail riding."

When she got off the phone, Pam wondered what she'd do while her friends were practicing. Was she going to spend all of spring vacation waiting around for Lulu and Anna while they rode with her mother and her riding students?

A little later, as Pam was fixing a picnic lunch for the trail ride, she heard a frightened whinny. At first she thought it was an injured horse being brought into her father's clinic for surgery. But when she heard the whinny a second time, she knew it came from Lightning's paddock. Pam ran out the kitchen door. In the middle of the field, she saw her pony rolling on the ground in pain.

Pam's father gave Lightning two shots, just like the day before. But this time it took longer to get the pony walking.

"She's even sicker than she was yesterday," Pam said.

"This is the second time it's happened to her," Dr. Crandal said. "I don't like that."

"What's making her sick, Dad?" Pam asked.

"If I didn't know better," he said, "I'd say this pony's been overeating." He looked around the paddock. "But there's not enough grass here for her to overgraze."

A car pulled into the parking area next to the animal clinic. "I have to get back to the clinic," he said. "Come get me if there's an emergency."

Pam felt lonely and discouraged as she led her pony around the paddock. Finally she saw Anna and Lulu coming off Pony Pal Trail.

When her friends reached her, Pam told them what had happened. "You guys should go ahead and practice with Mom," she said. "There's nothing you can do to help."

"I can't practice jumping when Lightning is sick again and we don't know why," Lulu said.

"There has to be *something* we can do," Anna said. "Let's think hard."

Pam kicked the ground with her foot. "I went over everything with my dad already," she said. Pam was about to kick the grass again, but stopped herself. On the ground, new grass and plants were just beginning to grow. "What about poisonous plants?" she said.

"Where?" Anna asked.

"Maybe growing right here in this paddock," Pam answered. "New plants we haven't noticed yet. You stay with Lightning," she told her friends. "I'll be right back."

Pam ran to her mother's office where there was a whole bookcase of books about horses. It didn't take her long to find exactly what she was looking for.

Back in the paddock, she showed Anna and Lulu two pages with pictures of plants poisonous to horses. "We'll check every inch of the paddock," she told them. "If we find a plant that looks like any of these, we'll dig it up."

The girls crawled up and down the field on their hands and knees.

Half an hour later, they'd finished their search without finding one poisonous plant. They sat on the ground and leaned against the paddock fence to rest. Pam saw that Lightning was standing in her favorite spot under the sugar maple tree. Her head was drooping.

"Lightning doesn't seem like herself," she said.

"Getting sick two days in a row has made her weak," Dr. Crandal said.

The girls looked up to see Pam's dad standing behind them on the other side of the fence.

"What can we do for her?" Pam asked.

"If she's not better tomorrow I'll run some more tests," he said. "All you can do right now is keep an eye on her."

After he left, Lulu turned to Pam and Anna. "What your dad just said reminds me of something my dad's always saying."

"What?" Pam asked.

" 'If you want to know how an animal lives, you have to watch the animal twenty-four hours a day.' Once my dad and another guy followed a group of gorillas to do this article for a nature magazine. At night they took turns sleeping so one of them would always be watching the gorillas."

"Even when the gorillas were sleeping?" Anna asked.

"Yup," Lulu said.

"Are you saying we should watch Lightning every second for twenty-four hours?" Pam asked.

"Yup," Lulu repeated.

"That's a *great* idea, Lulu," Pam said. "Then I'd know if she's doing something that makes her sick."

"What about at night?" Anna asked. "Pam can't stay awake all night long."

"If we have a barn sleepover," Lulu said, "we could take turns."

Pam was happy that her friends were trying so hard to help Lightning. And she was happy that they and their ponies would be staying for a sleepover.

But Pam was still sad. What if the Pony Pals couldn't figure out what was making Lightning sick? What if tomorrow Lightning got sick again? Or worse?

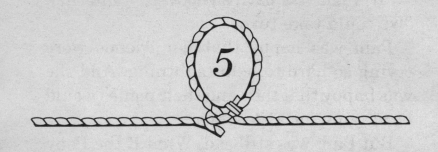

Pony Watch

That evening the Pony Pals ate a picnic dinner on the big flat rock at the far edge of the paddock. From there they could see their ponies and keep a special watch over Lightning.

"We've watched Lightning for eight hours so far," Pam said. "And she hasn't done anything that would make her sick."

The rock was flat enough for the checkerboard, so that's what the girls did next. "Just be sure one of us is always looking

at Lightning," Pam reminded her fellow detectives.

At nine o'clock Dr. Crandal came out to check on Lightning. He told the girls that she was recovering very well. "But I'd still like to know what gave her colic," he said. He gave Pam a kiss good night and said to the Pony Pals, "You all get a good night's sleep." Woolie was sniffing at his legs. "Come on, fella," he said. "Time to go in."

"Woolie can sleep with us tonight," Pam said. The dog yapped excitedly, as if he understood that he wouldn't be sleeping alone in the kitchen.

When Dr. Crandal left, the Pony Pals and Woolie went into Mrs. Crandal's office in the barn. They'd chosen the office as their "post" because of the room's big window facing the paddock.

Pam put a small clock and a piece of paper on the desk. "Here's the overnight schedule," she said.

PONY WATCH

9:00 P.M.	12:00 midnight	Anna's turn
12:01 A.M.	3:00 A.M.	Lulu's turn
3:01 A.M.	6:00 A.M.	Pam's turn

"Wouldn't it be easier if we just put Lightning in a stall for the night?" Anna asked.

"Sleeping in the barn isn't what Lightning normally does," Lulu said. "We're not changing what she does. We're spying to see if she starts to do something that could make her sick."

"Besides," Pam added, "Lightning likes to sleep outdoors."

Anna sat on the desk and looked out the window. "You guys should go to sleep while I watch," she said.

Pam and Lulu laid out their sleeping bags and scrunched into them.

Pam watched Anna put on her Walkman headphones. Because Anna didn't read very well, she sometimes listened to

37

books on tape. During their all-night Pony Watch, the Pony Pals were going to take turns listening to *Black Beauty*, the famous novel by Anna Sewell. It was a perfect way to stay awake.

Pam could hear from Lulu's breathing that she was definitely asleep. So was Woolie, who was curled up between them. Pam was feeling pretty sleepy herself. She turned over and faced the wall.

By the moonlight, Pam could make out all the horse-show ribbons hanging there. To help her fall asleep she began to count them the way some people count sheep. One, two, three, four, five. . . . She got all the way to forty-nine before she closed her eyes. The next thing she knew, Lulu was waking her up.

Pam wiggled out of her sleeping bag, stepped over the sleeping dog, and went over to her mother's desk to take Lulu's place.

"Did you see anything?" Pam whispered.

"Lightning's been standing under the

tree sleeping the whole time," Lulu answered. "During Anna's watch, too." She
handed Pam the Walkman and earphones.
"*Black Beauty* is great. It made me cry."

For the next two and a half hours Pam
stared at her own pony while listening to
the sad, wonderful story of a horse. Just
when things got better for Black Beauty,
his life would change from good to bad.

Pam was watching the sun rising behind
her own beautiful pony. Suddenly, Lightning woke up and ran across the paddock,
out of sight. Pam pulled off the earphones
and shouted, "Something's happening!"

She raced from the barn with Woolie at
her heels. Behind her she could hear Anna
and Lulu scrambling out of their sleeping
bags.

As Pam bolted out of the barn, she saw
that someone was at the paddock fence.
Lightning was there, too. The person was
holding a bag in one hand and offering
Lightning something to eat with the other
hand.

"Stop!" Pam screamed as she ran toward them. Woolie raced ahead and barked his loudest, fiercest bark.

Pam could see now that the person was a girl. The girl dropped the bag and jumped on her bike. Pam and Woolie chased her down Riddle Road, but the girl pedaled away faster than either of them could run. She turned the bend in the road and was out of sight.

When Anna and Lulu reached Riddle Road, Pam breathlessly told them, "Someone was feeding Lightning. Maybe poison."

Acorn and Snow White were at the fence with Lightning. The three ponies were sticking their noses under the fence. They wanted whatever that girl had dropped. Pam ran over and kicked the brown bag out of their reach.

The Pony Pals squatted around the bag.

"Don't touch it," Lulu warned. "We might mess up the girl's fingerprints. That's evidence."

Anna poked the bag with a stick so they could see inside.

"It's only some apples," Lulu said.

Pam's mother and father had come out to the paddock. "What's all the racket?" her father asked.

"What's going on?" her mother asked.

"We know why Lightning's been getting sick," Pam answered. "Someone's been feeding her poisoned apples."

The Racing Bike

"Maybe I should stay outside in case she comes back," Pam said, as she followed her parents and friends into the kitchen.

"She's not coming back so fast," Anna said. "You and Woolie really scared her."

Holding the bag by a corner, Pam dumped the apples onto the table.

"How could an apple be poisoned?" Lulu asked.

"Remember the story of Snow White?" Anna said. "One bite of an apple put her to sleep for about a million years."

"They smell like regular apples," Pam said.

Dr. Crandal studied them, too. He told the girls that while the apples were a little old, there was nothing about them that would make a pony sick.

"Unless," he said, "Lightning ate three or four apples in addition to her regular diet."

"If that girl fed Lightning apples yesterday and the day before, too," Pam said, "could that be what made her sick?"

"Most definitely," Dr. Crandal answered. "I'd say you girls solved the mystery of why Lightning is getting sick. She's been overeating."

"Congratulations, girls," Mrs. Crandal said. "You probably saved Lightning's life."

The Pony Pals didn't hit high fives or congratulate one another the way they usually did. They were very quiet. Instead of feeling proud and happy, they were feeling frightened. Frightened at the thought of how close Lightning had come to dying.

"Now we've got to make sure that girl never, ever, gets near Lightning," Pam whispered.

Mrs. Crandal handed Pam a pile of cereal bowls to put on the table. "During the day Lightning will be with you girls," Pam's mother said. "So she's safe for now. And maybe at night she should stay in the barn."

But what about when I have to go back to school? Pam thought. She had to find that girl.

"This morning let's get some of the winter coats off our ponies," Lulu said. "Then this afternoon we can go on a trail ride."

"Great idea, Lulu," Anna said. "And I'm going to trim Acorn's tail. He'll be so beautiful for the horse show."

"And don't forget, girls," Mrs. Crandal said, "there's a riding lesson for the show at ten." She turned to Pam. "Now that Lightning's better maybe you'll join us."

"No thanks," Pam said.

After breakfast the Pony Pals went out to the paddock and fed their ponies. Then they cleaned up Mrs. Crandal's office from the sleepover and did Pam's barn chores. Finally, they were ready for the big grooming session.

Their ponies loved to be groomed, so it was never a problem to keep them still. "Let's all do all three of them at the same time," Anna suggested. "I'll do manes and tails."

"And I'll use the shedding blade," Pam said.

"I'll follow you with the currycomb," Lulu added.

"Then we'll all do the final brushing," Anna said.

As the Pony Pals gave the ponies their six-hands grooming special, they talked about the mystery girl who had been feeding Lightning.

They agreed that for Lightning's safety

they had to find the girl. Pam needed to know for sure if she had fed Lightning before. "I want to be positively sure that overeating is what's making her sick," Pam said.

"And we should tell her to never, ever, do it again," Lulu added. "To Lightning or any other pony."

"How are we going to find her?" Anna asked.

"We have to remember everything we can about her," Lulu answered. "Especially you, Pam, because you saw her best."

"She's tall," Pam said. "Taller than any of us. So she's probably older than we are. She's probably Anna's sister's age. But not an adult. And I think I saw red hair sticking out from under her bike helmet."

"A redhead," Lulu said. "That should make her easier to find."

"And her bike is special," Pam recalled. "A fancy racing bike. It's black."

"A black racing bike," Anna said. "I think I've seen something like that around town."

"Where?" Pam asked.

"I don't know," Anna said. "It's just this feeling I have."

The five-year-old Crandal twins, Jack and Jill, came running across the paddock to where the Pony Pals were finishing Snow White's grooming. "Mom says — " Jack shouted.

"Mom says," Jill repeated when they reached the girls and their ponies.

Jack breathlessly completed the sentence, " — that it's time to practice for the horse show."

"Right," said Jill.

"We haven't finished grooming Lightning," Anna said.

"You guys go ahead," Pam said. "I'll finish her myself."

While Pam groomed her pony, she listened to the sounds coming from the outdoor rink where her best friends and her mother's students were riding. Pam remembered her first and only horse show. Everyone had expected her to do great because she was the teacher's daughter and had been riding since she was real little. But she did the worst of all her mother's students. She hadn't won any ribbons. It was nerve-racking and embarrassing to be in horse shows. How could anyone think it was fun?

Pam rubbed Lightning's coat with a clear cloth until it shined. It was so good to know Lightning was healthy again. But she would only stay healthy if Pam could find that girl and tell her to stop feeding Lightning apples.

Pam could see that the riding lesson was still going on in the rink. She wondered why Lulu and Anna had stopped and were cantering their ponies toward her.

Anna reached Pam first. After she halted, she leaned over in the saddle. "I remember

where I saw that fancy racing bike."

"You know the mystery girl?" Pam said.

"No," Anna answered. "But I know where to find her."

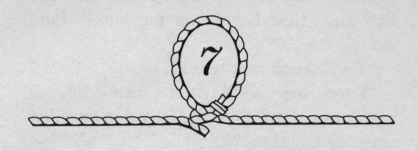

Stop!

A few minutes later, the Pony Pals were on Pony Pal Trail. They started talking about how to catch the girl.

"I've only seen the bike a couple of times," Anna said. "And that was early in the morning."

"How early?" Pam asked.

"Around seven. I saw her from my bedroom window. I noticed because it was so early and the bike went by so fast, like in a race."

"Were the two days you saw her the two days that Lightning got sick?" Pam asked.

"Yes," Anna answered.

"Those are the days she came by our place, too," Pam said. "So why don't we just wait for her there?"

"I don't think she'll go on Riddle Road again," Lulu said. "Not after we all yelled at her and everything."

"She's probably afraid of Woolie," Anna added. "People on bikes don't like dogs coming after them."

"We should wait for her on Main Street tomorrow morning," Lulu said.

With Anna leading the way, they turned off Pony Pal Trail onto a trail that led to the Wiggins Estate. Acorn whinnied happily. All the ponies put more energy into their walk. They loved to go into the Wiggins Estate with its great woodland trails and big fields.

"You should come to my house early tomorrow morning," Anna said. "We'll wait for the girl on Main Street."

"How are we going to get her to stop?" Lulu asked.

"She really speeds on that bike," Pam said.

"I've got an idea," Anna said. "Let's make a big sign. We'll stand by the side of the road and hold it up."

"Great," Pam said.

"It should be just a few words so it's easy to read," Lulu said.

"What's it going to say?" Anna asked.

"Something to trick her into stopping," Lulu suggested. "How about, You Won a Big Prize!?"

"She'd never believe that," Pam said.

They'd reached the edge of two big open fields divided by a low stone wall. This was one of the Pony Pals' favorite spots for galloping and jumping. "Let's work our ponies here for a while," Lulu suggested.

Anna and Lulu galloped and jumped

their ponies around the field three times. But Pam jumped only once because Lightning had just been sick. While she and Lightning watched the others, Pam tried to think of what the sign should say. You HURT MY PONY! was her first idea. But she knew that wasn't very good. Neither was, I'LL HAVE YOU ARRESTED IF YOU DON'T STOP FEEDING MY PONY. She hoped that Lulu and Anna would have some better ideas.

The Pony Pals stopped to rest and let the ponies drink from Badd Brook. Sitting on the rocks by the water, they talked about their ideas for what the sign should say.

Lulu and Anna agreed that Pam's ideas sounded too angry.

Anna wanted to draw a picture of a dead pony surrounded by apples. Pam and Lulu thought that would be too hard for a girl riding by on a bike to see.

But Lulu had another idea that they all agreed was perfect.

"I can make the sign tonight," Anna said. "I've got lots of art supplies."

"When we get home I'll write the words down for you," Lulu offered. "So you don't make any spelling mistakes."

The next morning Pam woke with a real alarm clock instead of her Woolie bark-alarm. She was getting up an hour earlier than usual. By five-thirty she was out in the paddock, keeping an eye on Riddle Road, just in case the girl did come by and try to feed Lightning again. She didn't.

Then Pam fed Lightning and did her morning chores. By six-fifteen she was riding onto Pony Pal Trail in the early morning mist.

Cantering on the dirt path between the tall trees, Pam thought about what life was like in the time of Black Beauty. There were no trucks, tractors, or cars. Horses, not machines, plowed fields. I wish I had lived in those times, Pam thought. I bet back then people weren't wasting their time in dumb horse shows, competing for a bunch of stupid ribbons. They needed horses for important things.

By six-thirty Pam rode up to the Harley paddock. Anna and Lulu were waiting for her. They helped her unsaddle Lightning and put her in the paddock with Acorn and Snow White. Then the Pony Pals went to Main Street and stood at the edge of the town green with their sign.

"What if she sees us and goes the other way?" Lulu asked.

"Or whizzes right past us," Anna added. "We could never catch her."

"We'd better smile and look friendly," Lulu suggested. "That way she'll know we're nice."

"I can't smile," Pam said. "I'm too mad at her."

"Do it for Lightning," Anna suggested.

"Okay," Pam agreed.

Just then they saw the girl speeding up

Main Street on her racing bike.

The Pony Pals put on their brightest smiles and held up the sign. It read:

STOP. MUST TALK TO YOU. VERY IMPORTANT.

The biker was so focused on pedaling fast, she didn't notice them or the sign.

Pam yelled out, "Hey! Look!"

The girl turned her head in their direction and screeched her bike to a stop. Pam saw that the girl was looking at a stopwatch. The Pony Pals ran over to her. She was out of breath when she spoke. "I was having my best time ever," she said. "This had better be important."

"It is," Pam said.

"You're the kid who scared me yesterday," the girl said to Pam. She read the sign that was now on the ground. "What's all this?" she asked. "Is this some silly game?"

"It's not a game," Pam said angrily. "You almost killed my pony."

"Don't be ridiculous," the girl said.

"It's true," Anna said. "You gave Lightning apples."

"Horses love apples," the girl said. "Give me a break."

"It was too much food with all the other stuff she eats," Lulu said. "Lightning got really sick."

"And she almost died," Pam added.

The girl was looking at them as if they were crazy. "Why should I believe you?" she asked. "You're some bored kids who don't have enough to do on vacation. And you've ruined my practice session."

Pam felt tears forming in her eyes, but she was determined not to cry. If she cried the girl would really think they were babies and *never* believe them. Then she might continue overfeeding horses. Maybe even Lightning.

"Look, we're not going to get you into trouble or anything," Pam said. "But you've got to understand. If horses eat too much they get very, very sick. They can't throw up."

"Can't throw up?" the girl laughed. "Now I really know you're fooling around. I'm out of here." She got on her bike to ride off. "And don't ever bother me again."

The Gift

The Pony Pals knew that they couldn't let the girl get away. Anna grabbed the front wheel of the girl's bike and Lulu grabbed the back wheel.

"Let go of my bike," the girl said.

Anna and Lulu held on tight.

"Right now!" the girl shouted. "You'll throw off the alignment."

Anna and Lulu didn't let go.

"Little kids can be such a pain!" the girl exclaimed.

"We'll let go, if you promise not to ride away," Anna said.

"Okay, I promise," the girl said.

Pam pointed to a bench on the town green. "Let's go over there."

"Only for a minute," the girl said.

Pam and the girl sat on the bench. Anna and Lulu leaned on the fence facing them.

"You know all about bikes, right?" Pam asked.

"Sure I do," the girl answered. "I'm a state champion in distance racing. There's a big Eastern Division race next week and you've just ruined my practice run — and the alignment on my bike."

"You know all about bikes," Pam said. "Well, we know all about ponies."

"Pam's father's a veterinarian," Lulu added.

"And we all know that if horses overeat, it can make them very sick," Pam continued.

"Because they can't throw up?" the girl asked with a laugh.

Anna spoke in her most serious voice, "It may sound funny to you that horses don't throw up. But, for horses, it's not funny at all."

The girl looked around at the Pony Pals. She turned serious herself. "You guys are telling the truth, aren't you?" she said. "About the throwing-up stuff and about the pony being sick."

They all nodded solemnly.

The girl took off her helmet. She had the reddest hair that Pam had ever seen. "By the way," the girl said, "I'm Diane Mc-Gann."

The Pony Pals introduced themselves, too.

Diane wasn't mad at them anymore for interrupting her ride. She seemed a little frightened when she asked, "Did I really make that beautiful pony sick?"

The three girls nodded again.

"How many times did you feed her?" Pam asked.

"Twice before the time you stopped me,"

Diane answered. "Your pony's so beautiful that I started bringing her apples. That way she'd come and stay with me awhile. I really made her sick?"

"It wasn't your fault," Anna said. "It's not like the wicked queen in Snow White. You didn't know any better. And the apples weren't poisoned. We checked."

"I'd never hurt an animal on purpose," Diane said. "Even a dog that's barking at me when I'm riding on my bike. I never kick at them like some people do." Pam could see that Diane was upset. "Was your pony *very* sick?" she asked.

"*Very*," Pam said. "If it had happened again Lightning could have died."

Diane was silent for a few seconds. Then she asked, "How does she feel now?"

"My dad said she'll probably be okay as long as she doesn't overeat again. I can't ride her too much for a couple of days."

"She's not a hundred percent better then," Diane said.

"Promise me you'll never ever feed her again," Pam said.

"Of course I won't," Diane answered. "I'm just worried she won't get all better."

The town clock struck the half hour. "It's seven-thirty," Diane said. She got up and put her helmet back on. "I've got to get to the gym for my workout," she said. "My coach is waiting for me. He'll think I had an accident or something."

She got on her bike. "Don't worry," she told Pam, "I'll never feed her again." She rode off the green and up Main Street.

When she was out of sight, the Pony Pals jumped up, hit high fives, and shouted, "All *right!*" Then they went to Off-Main Diner to celebrate.

The Pony Pals were glad to see that their favorite booth in the back was empty.

"Mom said we don't have to pay for breakfast," Anna said, "because of vacation and everything. But we have to take our own orders."

Pam took a pad and pencil off the counter and took the orders.

Anna ordered blueberry pancakes. Lulu wanted Granola with banana and strawberries. Pam wrote down, "scrambled eggs with ham and homefries," for herself.

While the Pony Pals were eating, they congratulated themselves again about how they got Diane McGann to stop and listen to them. They all agreed that she was totally innocent of any crime against Lightning.

"She's really sorry about what she did," Pam said. "I could tell."

Anna waved toward the door of the diner. "Look," she told Lulu and Pam. "Ms. Wiggins just came in."

When Ms. Wiggins saw the Pony Pals, she came right over to their booth. They all liked Ms. Wiggins, especially Anna. And Ms. Wiggins loved horses as much as they did. She still had her Shetland pony she rode as a young girl. The Pony Pals usually didn't visit Ms. Wiggins when they rode on her trails on Wiggins Estate. They knew that she liked to be alone to do her paintings. But sometimes Ms. Wiggins left her big house and property to eat at the diner. Like everyone in town, she loved the food at Off-Main Diner.

"Well, well," Ms. Wiggins said, "I'm so glad to see you all here." She held out three packages wrapped in colorfully decorated brown paper. "Anna, I thought I'd have your mother give you these. Now I can do it myself." She handed each of the girls a gift.

"You open yours first, Anna," Lulu said.

Anna carefully opened the gift so the hand-painted paper wouldn't tear. She held up a periwinkle-blue satin vest. "Oh-hh, it's beautiful," Anna exclaimed.

"I made it plenty big," Ms. Wiggins said, "so you can wear it over a jacket. It's for the horse show."

Lulu opened her package. She got a vest,

too. "I love it," she said as she slipped the vest on. "Thank you so much."

Pam unwrapped her gift, but she didn't unfold the vest.

Mrs. Harley and the waiter, Fred, came over to the booth. Everyone in the diner was stretching their necks to get a look at the vests.

"Mom, you told her our color, didn't you?" Anna said.

Mrs. Harley smiled and nodded.

"Then I remembered this fabric," Ms. Wiggins told them. "It's been hanging around my place for years. I guess it was just waiting to become vests for the Pony Pals."

"They're perfect," Lulu said. "Thank you."

Anna jumped up and gave Ms. Wiggins a hug. "Thank you," she said. "Thank you."

"Are you coming to the show?" Lulu asked Ms. Wiggins.

"Absolutely," she answered. "Winston

and I are giving the younger children cart rides. My old pony loves to be in horse shows and I do, too. I'm particularly looking forward to seeing you three girls there."

"Thank you for the vest, it's very pretty," Pam said to Ms. Wiggins. "But I'm not going to be in the horse show."

The Chicken-Pox Horse Show

The day before the horse show, the Pony Pals met at the Harley paddock.

"Where are we going to trail ride today?" Pam asked.

"Let's ride over to Olson's farm," Anna suggested. "I want to see how long it will take to get there from my house."

"Great idea," Lulu said. "Snow White can see the ring. That way the farm won't be strange for her tomorrow."

Pam agreed to the plan. "I like the trail to Olson's," she said.

"Did you tell your parents how we solved the mystery of the apple feeder?" Anna asked Pam.

"Yes," Pam answered. "They think we'd all make great detectives."

The Pony Pals rode along Main Street. Then they made a right onto Belgo Road. Suddenly Snow White threw her head back. "Whoa, girl," Lulu said. As Lulu calmed down her pony, Pam and Anna looked around to see what had spooked Snow White.

They saw Diane McGann riding her bike up from behind them.

"Hi," Diane said as she rode alongside them.

They all said hi back to her.

"Don't ride your bike close to horses," Pam said. "It could scare them."

"Sorry," Diane said as she got off her bike. "How's Lightning doing?" she asked Pam. "She looks okay."

"She's all right now," Pam said.

"I've been so worried about her," Diane said. "It's all I've been thinking about."

They'd passed Off-Main Diner and reached the turnoff for the trail. When the Pony Pals halted their ponies, Diane stopped, too.

"Where are you all going now?" she asked.

"Over to Olson's farm," Anna answered.

"We're in a horse show there tomorrow," Lulu explained.

"Good for you," Diane said. "I'm going to be in a big bike race myself next weekend. In Virginia."

Through tension in the reins, Pam could feel that Lightning wanted to go over to Diane. Lightning wants to see if she has any of those apples on her, Pam thought. She held back her pony.

"I've never seen anyone ride a bike as fast as you do," Anna said.

Diane wasn't paying attention to what Anna was saying. She was looking at

Lightning. "Can I pat her on the neck?" she asked Pam.

"Sure," Pam said. "That won't hurt her."

Diane walked up to Lightning and rubbed the smooth reddish-brown length of Lightning's neck.

"I'm going to go to that horse show," Diane said, "so I can see for sure that Lightning is okay."

"Don't you have to practice bike racing?" Pam asked.

"I can take a few hours off," Diane said. She scratched the white upside-down heart on Lightning's forehead. "I don't think I'm going to win in Virginia anyway," she said. "I haven't been riding very well this week."

"Lightning's not going to be in the horse show," Pam said.

Diane looked up at Pam with alarm. "I thought she was all better."

"We just don't like to be in horse shows," Pam answered.

A red motor scooter whizzed down Main Street. "Uh-oh," Diane said. "That was my coach. I'm on the wrong road and I shouldn't have stopped. Now I've got to try to catch up to him."

She got on her bike and sped off.

"She still doesn't believe that Lightning's okay," Anna said.

"I know," Pam said.

The Olson farm was a busy place that day. People were setting up jumps and decorating them with potted flowers. Volunteer firemen were unloading a big barbecue pit from the back of a pickup truck. And Pam's mother and Mr. Olson were giving directions for putting up the judges' stands. Another woman was installing a loudspeaker system for the ringmasters.

"I can't wait for tomorrow," Anna said. "I think Acorn's going to do really well."

"You and Acorn looked great in practice," Lulu told her.

"You and Snow White did, too," Anna said.

Pam felt unhappy. She was remembering that the only horse show she'd been in was held right here, at Olson's farm. She wanted to get away as fast as she could.

"Let's go," she told her friends.

"Okay," Lulu said.

"We can go back to my place," Anna said, "and make the rest of our decorations for tomorrow. Will you help us, Pam?"

"Sure," Pam said. "Why not?"

Even though it was her turn to lead on the trail, Pam was feeling depressed and wanted to be last. She told Lulu to take her place.

Later, in Anna's bedroom, the girls wrapped blue and silver ribbon around Anna's and Lulu's riding crops. Then they stuck periwinkle-blue stars on the outside edge of their saddle blankets and on the bands of their helmets.

"Pam, this would be so much more fun if you were going to be in the show, too," Lulu said.

"I told you I hate horse shows," Pam told her. "I always have. Ever since I was little."

"She was only in one," Anna told Lulu. "The chicken-pox horse show."

"The chicken-pox horse show?" Lulu said. "What's that?"

"What are you talking about, Anna?" Pam asked.

"Don't you remember?" Anna said. "You came down with chicken pox during that horse show. You were the first one to get sick. Then I and just about everybody else in our riding class got chicken pox."

The Pony Pals were silent for a second. They were all remembering what it was like to have chicken pox.

"That's it," Lulu said.

"What?" Pam asked.

"Why you don't like to be in horse shows."

"Because of chicken pox?" Pam said. "That's not why. You don't understand. No one understands." She got up. "I'm going home."

Don't Stop!

"Pam, please stay," Lulu said.

Pam sat back down on the edge of Anna's bed.

"When I got chicken pox I felt awful," Lulu told her. "It was when Dad and I first moved to England. I kept telling him that I was miserable and that I hated England. It turned out I really loved England. What I hated was having chicken pox."

"I couldn't even *sit* on a horse when I had it," Anna said. "Pam, you got all those spots during a horse show."

"Don't you see?" Lulu added. "Chicken pox ruined the show for you."

Listening to her friends talk, Pam remembered the horse show better than ever before. Not just the part about not getting any ribbons. Now she remembered the part about chicken pox. After the show, when she took off her blouse, she saw that her belly was covered in itchy red spots. She also had a fever and felt very nervous. Just the way she felt during the horse show.

"How can you know what it feels like to be in a horse show if you had chicken pox during the only one you were ever in?" Lulu asked.

"I never thought about it that way," Pam answered.

"You hated chicken pox," Lulu and Anna said in unison.

"How can anybody compete when they're sick?" Lulu said.

"Please say you'll be in the show tomorrow," Anna pleaded.

"Your mother says you and Lightning

would do great in competition," Lulu said.

"She's your teacher," Anna added. "So she should know."

"I don't care what my mother thinks," Pam snapped. "I'm sick of everybody nagging me about horse shows and about being the teacher's daughter."

Anna put her arm around Pam's shoulder. "I just think you should give it another try," she said.

"You could enter the Pleasure Division where you do all the things we do when we trail ride," Lulu suggested.

"Like opening and closing gates," Anna added. "And jumping over logs. Just pretend you're on a trail ride and you won't be nervous," Lulu said.

"Okay," Pam finally agreed. "I'll be in the horse show."

Anna and Lulu raised their hands to do a high five. But Pam stopped them. "Wait a minute," she said. "Okay . . . I'll be in the horse show *if* you help me do something first."

When Anna and Lulu heard what Pam wanted them to do, they happily agreed. Then the Pony Pals all raised their hands, shouted "All *right!*" and hit their high fives.

The next morning, Pam woke up before her Woolie bark-alarm again. It was still dark outside while she dressed and ate a bowl of cereal. But by the time she'd fed Lightning and saddled her, the sun was coming up.

"We're going to be in a horse show today," she told her pony. "I was sick during the last horse show I was in. But today I'm healthy. And so are you."

Lightning nickered and nudged Pam's shoulder.

Lulu and Anna were waiting for Pam at the other end of Pony Pal Trail. Anna held three cardboard signs. Each one was sta-

pled to a stick. Pam unsaddled Lightning and let her into the paddock with Snow White and Acorn. Then Anna passed out the signs.

"Okay," Pam said. "Let's go."

The three girls went on to Main Street and waited. And waited.

"What if she doesn't come this way today?" Lulu asked.

"She'll come," Pam said. "She's probably just riding slower today."

A minute later the Pony Pals saw Diane McGann pumping her bike up Main Street.

"She's not taking the hill very fast," Anna said.

"Maybe she's feeling awful that she made my pony sick and is worried that Lightning's not better," Pam said. She thought about how lonely it must be for Diane to ride her bike all by herself for hours at a time. And she thought about how lucky she was to have great pony-riding friends.

When Diane got to the top of the hill, she

looked up and saw the Pony Pals. They held up their cardboard signs.

Anna's sign read:

DON'T STOP!

Lulu's sign read:

KEEP RIDING!

And Pam's sign read:

LIGHTNING IN HORSE SHOW!

Diane read the signs as she slowly rode by the girls. Her face lit up with a big smile.

"Come on, Diane!" Anna shouted. "You can do it."

Diane looked at the road ahead of her.

"You're a winner, Diane!" Lulu called out. "Go for it."

Diane started pedaling harder.

"Do it for Lightning!" Pam shouted.

Diane didn't even turn around. She was totally concentrating on biking as she sped out of sight.

The Parade

The Pony Pals went back to the Harley paddock to give their ponies a final grooming for the horse show. Lulu's grandmother, who was a hairdresser, walked across the paddock toward them.

"It's a special day," she told them. "I thought you could use my professional services."

The girls were all surprised because they knew that Grandmother Sanders didn't like horses very much. But she was very cheerful as she taught the Pony Pals how to braid periwinkle-blue yarn into their ponies' manes.

After Grandmother Sanders left, the girls painted the ponies' hooves with oil. And Pam washed Lightning's upside-down heart so it would shine. She thought about the first time she saw that white marking, and how much she loved her pony. "I can't wait to show everyone at the horse show what a wonderful pony Lightning is," she told her friends.

The Pony Pals mounted their ponies for the ride over to Olson's. "Look," Anna said, "the sky is the same shade of blue as our vests and decorations."

Pam looked at the periwinkle-blue sky, and smiled. The Pony Pals were on their way to the horse show and she felt great.

"You know," she said to her friends, "I feel a lot different than I did the first time I was going to a horse show. This is *fun*."

Anna and Lulu smiled at one another, but they *didn't* say, "I told you so."

Olson's farm was bustling with people and horses. Everywhere she looked, Pam saw horses. There were horses being led out of trailers, horses being ridden across the field, horses on leads. The Pony Pals dismounted and led their ponies over to the registration table.

After they had registered, they looked at the schedule of classes in their programs.

"My Pony Hunter classes are in Ring Two," Lulu said. "Anna's Short Stirrup classes are in Ring One."

Pam saw that her class, Open Pleasure Pony, was also in Ring One. "It looks like we'll be running back and forth between the rings if we want to see one another," she said.

"And sometimes we'll be competing at the same time," Lulu added.

"Ten minutes until the first class," Mr. Olson announced.

Pam was feeling a little nervous. But not

the kind of nervous that made her unhappy. It was the kind of nervous that made her feel excited.

First she watched Anna and Acorn win a second-place ribbon for Short Stirrup Equitation over fences. Then she watched Lulu in Ring Two in Pony Hunter over fences. Lulu and Snow White won a first-place blue ribbon.

"Rema will be so happy," Lulu told Pam.

When it was time for Open Pleasure Pony, Pam told Lightning, "It's just like being on a trail ride. We'll do just fine."

And so they did.

Mrs. Crandal came up to Pam as she was exiting the ring with a red ribbon on Lightning's bridle. Pam figured her mother would say how proud she was of her and that she knew all along that she would do well in horse shows. But she didn't. Instead, her mother said, "You know, Pam, I'm very happy you're in the horse show. Not because I expect you to win ribbons. But because I think horse shows are a fun part of being a rider. Are you having a good time?"

"Yes," Pam admitted. She leaned over and patted Lightning on the neck. "Lightning is, too."

Mrs. Crandal scratched Lightning's head. "Congratulations to both of you," she said.

"Thanks, Mom," Pam said. Pam was glad that her mother understood. Then her mother went off to Ring Two to help her students.

As she dismounted, Pam saw Diane McGann walking toward her. "I didn't even know you were here," Pam told Diane.

"I got here just in time to see you," Diane told her. "Lightning looks so beautiful with all the blue decorations. And the way you jumped over the stone wall! It was all terrific. Congratulations."

"Do you see how healthy Lightning is?" Pam asked.

Diane smiled. "I finally believe she's

okay," she said. "I felt just awful before."

"I know," Pam said. "How was your bike ride this morning?"

"Better," she answered. "I picked up some speed after you guys cheered me on." She looked around at all the horse show activity. "Being here reminds me of how much fun bike races can be," she said. "That's when I get to be with other racers. We have lots of fun, too."

"Pony Hunter Under Saddle in Ring Two," the loudspeaker announced.

"Do you want to watch Lulu and Snow White jump?" Pam asked Diane.

Diane stroked Lightning's cheek. "I can't," she said. "I need to clock another thirty miles on my bike this afternoon."

Pam said, "Oh, that's too bad."

"No it's not," Diane said. "I have a race to win next week and I want to be ready. You all inspired me. Good luck with the rest of the show."

"Thanks," said Pam. "Bye."

Pam led Lightning over to Ring Two so

they could watch Lulu in her next class.

The afternoon at the horse show was as much fun as the morning. Pam made sure that Jack and Jill got cart rides with Ms. Wiggins and Winston. "I'm so glad you decided to be in the show." Ms. Wiggins told Pam.

"Me, too," Pam said. "Thanks again for the vest."

"I haven't seen the three of you together once today," Ms. Wiggins said. "But I expect before the day is over, I'll see you riding side by side."

"When?" Pam asked.

"You'll see," Ms. Wiggins answered with a wink.

After the last ribbons and the championship cups were awarded, Mr. Olson announced: "The ponies and horses in this competition are so beautifully turned out that we're going to have a parade." A lot of people cheered.

"You have ten minutes to line up behind the pony cart in Ring One," Mr. Olson continued. "Once around the ring and then over to Ring Two."

Pam saw that Ms. Wiggins was inviting the twins, Jack and Jill, to ride with her at the head of the parade. They were jumping up and down with excitement.

"And behind the pony cart," Mr. Olson was saying, "I'd like to see Pam Crandal, Anna Harley, and Lulu Sanders."

Pam straightened out the ribbons that decorated Lightning's bridle. Then she mounted and rode up alongside Anna and Lulu. Other riders and their horses lined up behind them.

Pam imagined how she would have felt if she hadn't been in the horse show. Lightning and I would have missed so much fun, she thought. And there would have been only two girls with periwinkle-blue colors.

"All right, let's go," Mr. Olson announced.

Suddenly, lively marching music filled the air. Lightning, Snow White, and Acorn

held their heads high and stepped out into a brisk walk. Pam loved how the three ponies were keeping in step with one another as they paraded around the ring.

Before the Pony Pals dismounted at the end of the parade, a woman with a camera came up to them. "I'm a reporter for the *County Times*," she said. "I'd love to get a picture."

The three girls sat proudly in their saddles and smiled at the camera. The reporter clicked off a few shots. Then she took out her notebook and pencil. "I need to know who you girls are, for the caption under the picture," she said.

Pam, Anna, and Lulu answered together. "We're the Pony Pals," they said.

Dear Reader:

I am having a lot of fun researching and writing books about the Pony Pals. I've met many interesting kids and adults who love ponies. And I've visited some wonderful ponies at homes, farms, and riding schools.

Before writing Pony Pals I wrote fourteen novels for children and young adults. Four of these were honored by Children's Choice Awards.

I live in Sharon, Connecticut, with my husband, Lee, and our dog, Willie. Our daughter is all grown up and has her own apartment in New York City.

Besides writing novels I like to draw, paint, garden, and swim. I didn't have a pony when I was growing up, but I have always loved them and dreamt about riding. Now I take riding lessons on a horse named Saz.

I like reading and writing about ponies as much as I do riding. Which proves to me that you don't have to ride a pony to love them. And you certainly don't need a pony to be a Pony Pal.

Happy Reading,

Jeanne Betancourt